Green Roof
Geese
Marylyen Jimenez-Ayala,
Alaysha Brunner, and Kathy McQuate

Green Roof Geese

Illustrated by the authors and Sydney McQuate.

This is a work of fiction based on a real family of Canada Geese who made a nest on the green roof of Linden-McKinley STEM Academy during the closure of Ohio schools beginning in March, 2020 due to COVID-19. Names, characters, places, and events are used fictitiously.

FIRST EDITION

The authors would like to extend a special thanks to all of the people who helped us research, read early drafts, or provided feedback: Aneysa Brown, Mary Brosovich, J'Quane Foxx, Mia Ott, Jamie Rhein, Alana Veach, Me'Asia Winston, Mahleyah Yisrael, the the Brunner Family, the Jimenez-Ayala family, McQuate family, the Schwamburger family, and the Welker family.

We would also like to thank the LMSA staff members who helped take care of our family of Canada Geese: Christian Angel, Duane Bland, Marilyn Chalfant, Steven Cudney, Kambie Harrison, Aneesa Hines, Paula Hughes, and Henry Lee.

It was spring,
and I was slowly growing taller.
Ever since I woke up in November,
there was noise all around me.

But for the last two weeks of March,
the middle school was quiet.
No kids.
No yelling or laughter.
No one bothering me or my tulip friends.
Just the way I liked it.

The roof was finally empty.
Then, I heard a loud sound.

"Ugh. What is going on out there?"
I looked around my pot,
but all I saw was dirt.

I knew this sound.
A goose was near the green roof.

I shouted, "Stay away from me!"
It landed anyway.

"You are *not* going to have me for dinner!"

A goose once nibbled on my bulb,
and I didn't bloom that year.

It sounded like the goose
was eating everything on the roof.

Crunch.
Crunch.

I was sure that I was next.
The bugs in my planter
always chewed on my leaves, but at least they were small. This goose sounded huge.

I could hear the goose breaking sticks
and munching on plants.
I said, “When those onions grow, this whole place will stink.
You better get out while you can.”

I still heard chewing, so I tried something more creative. "There are big monsters that live under the grass here. You *seriously* don't want to stay."

This continued for days.
Whatever I said, the goose still wouldn't leave me alone.

Eventually, I grew tall enough
that I was able to see more.
I was right! But it wasn't just one goose.
It was a pair of geese.
"Are you kidding me?" I said out loud.
My friends were still too far down in their pots
to be worried.

I noticed a mound of twigs and plants nearby.
"A nest? Oh no!" I moaned.
A nest meant more geese.

Of course without water and food,
those baby geese would die.
It hadn't rained for days.
The last thing I wanted
was to hear Mother Goose and Gander Goose
crying all night long because they weren't smart enough
to make a nest on the ground.

When Mother Goose was near my pot I yelled,
"You need to leave! Can't you see there is no water on this roof? Hey! Don't turn your back on me! Where are you going?"

She walked away from my pot
and over to her nest.

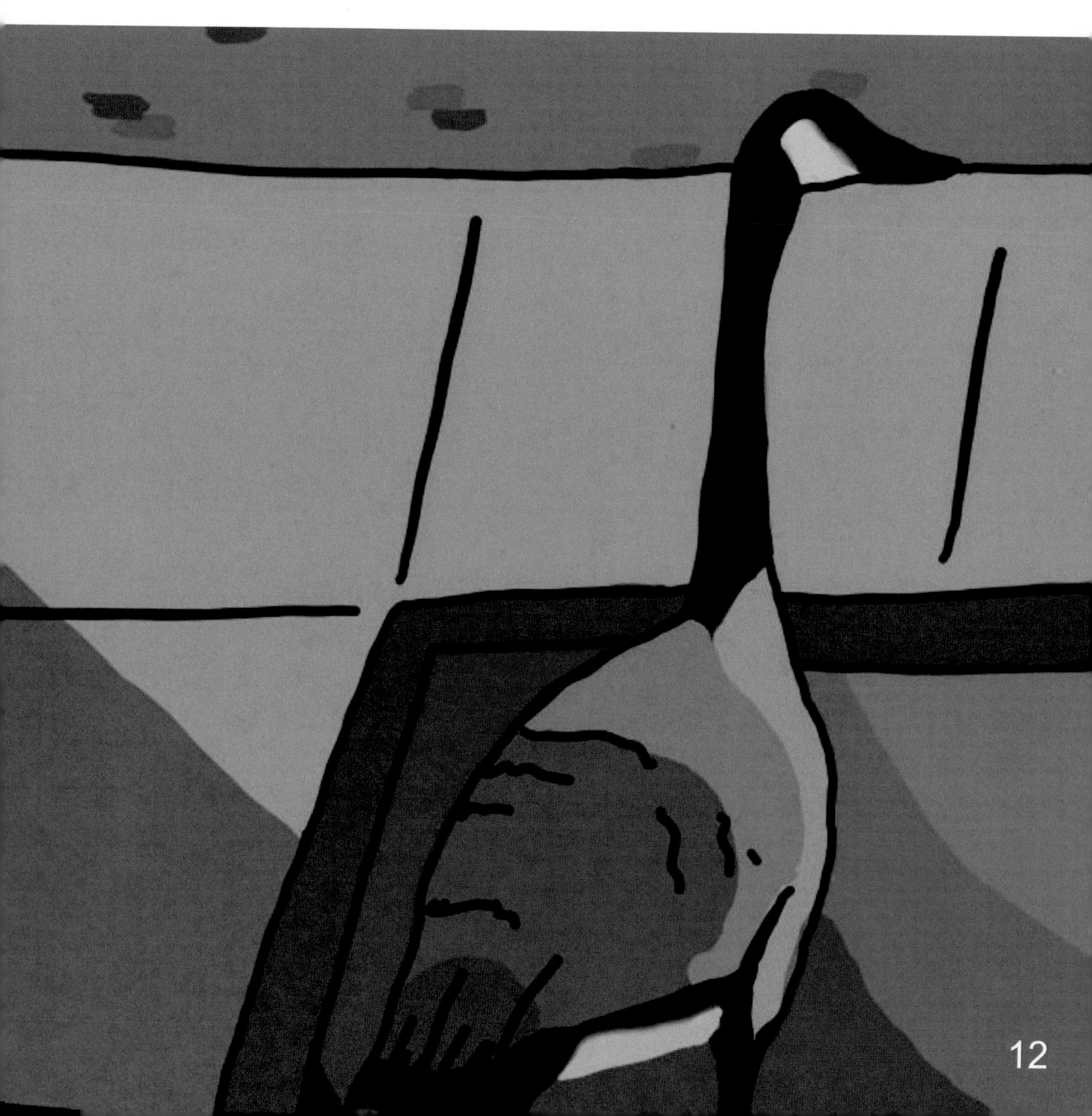

The next thing I knew, a large egg appeared. **Boop.**

It took her three days to lay two eggs. **Boop.**

By the end of the week, there were four.

Boop. **Boop.**

"We've got a big problem," I complained to my friends.

I saw Mother Goose sit on her eggs in the sun,
in the cold, and in the rain.
When she flew away to get food each day,
she covered the eggs with feathers.
Gander Goose, the father,
watched over the nest when she was gone.
Unfortunately, they were never gone long.

Four weeks of sitting went by
before I saw a crack in an egg.

There was a hole.
Then there was a bigger crack and a
bigger hole.

Peck.
Peck.

The gosling's beak poked out.
And then his head.
And then, he tried to get back in,
but the shell broke apart.
I called him Dresden.

I whispered to my friends, “I’m going to give them names, but it does *not* mean that I like them.”

Next, another gosling appeared.
She was fluffy and yellow,
and she had big feet like a duck,
so I decided to call her Duxberry.

Chirp.
Chirp.
Chirp.

Homestead was born third.
He didn't want to leave the nest. What a baby.

Blake was born last,
and she was fearless, just like me.
Her brothers and sister followed her everywhere.

While all of this hatching was happening,
I began to bloom.
I was finally tall enough to see the entire green roof,
which was no longer green.

Mother Goose and Gander Goose
had eaten almost all of the plants.

"Well, now I know where they get the phrase 'silly goose' from," I said to the tulips.

Mother Goose walked over to a large container.
She looked up at the pot.
She looked down at the goslings.
She looked up at the pot again.
They were not going to reach that food
any time soon.

She looked around and waddled over
to the middle of the green roof.
Her youngsters followed her
and found some shoots of grass
hiding in the succulents.
There was not enough food for six geese.

I saw a door open,
and a tall man came near us.
The geese froze.
He took out a phone.
When I realized that he was
taking pictures of me,
I started to pose.

A minute later, he was gone.
Then, I saw him looking through
the window.
He was staring, with shock,
at the geese.

"Great!" I said.
"Maybe he will help us
get rid of these geese
who moved in without
permission."

We had two hot days in a row
after the goslings were discovered,
and there was no water anywhere.
Mother Goose and Gander Goose were getting frantic.

They honked and honked at the goslings,
trying to get them to fly up and off the roof.
“These parents have no idea what they are doing,”
I said to the tulips. “Even I know that goslings can’t
fly until they are at least two months old.”

"These silly geese are going to die if we don't help them. We have to attract attention. It's time to bloom."

The next morning I woke up to another hot, dry day. The goslings did not look good. They were in a pile in the shade, and they didn't move much.

Then, I looked at the other tulips
and noticed they had all bloomed.

Tulips listen. Geese don't.
We are so much smarter than they are.

My friends were taller and more beautiful
than I had ever seen them.
Now, we just had to wait
and hope that someone would see us through the windows
and want to get closer.

Sure enough,
a group of people showed up a few days later
with a container of water and some grass.

They all had masks on
which made them look like very large geese.
It was funny.

Visitors continued to come every few days,
and I continued to watch the annoying geese.

I found myself thinking,
"The parents are loud and eat too much,
but the goslings are kind of cute."

One day when the water container was empty,
Blake wandered around
and headed towards the greenhouse.
The greenhouse was scary.
It made loud noises when the wind blew,
and part of the roof was missing.

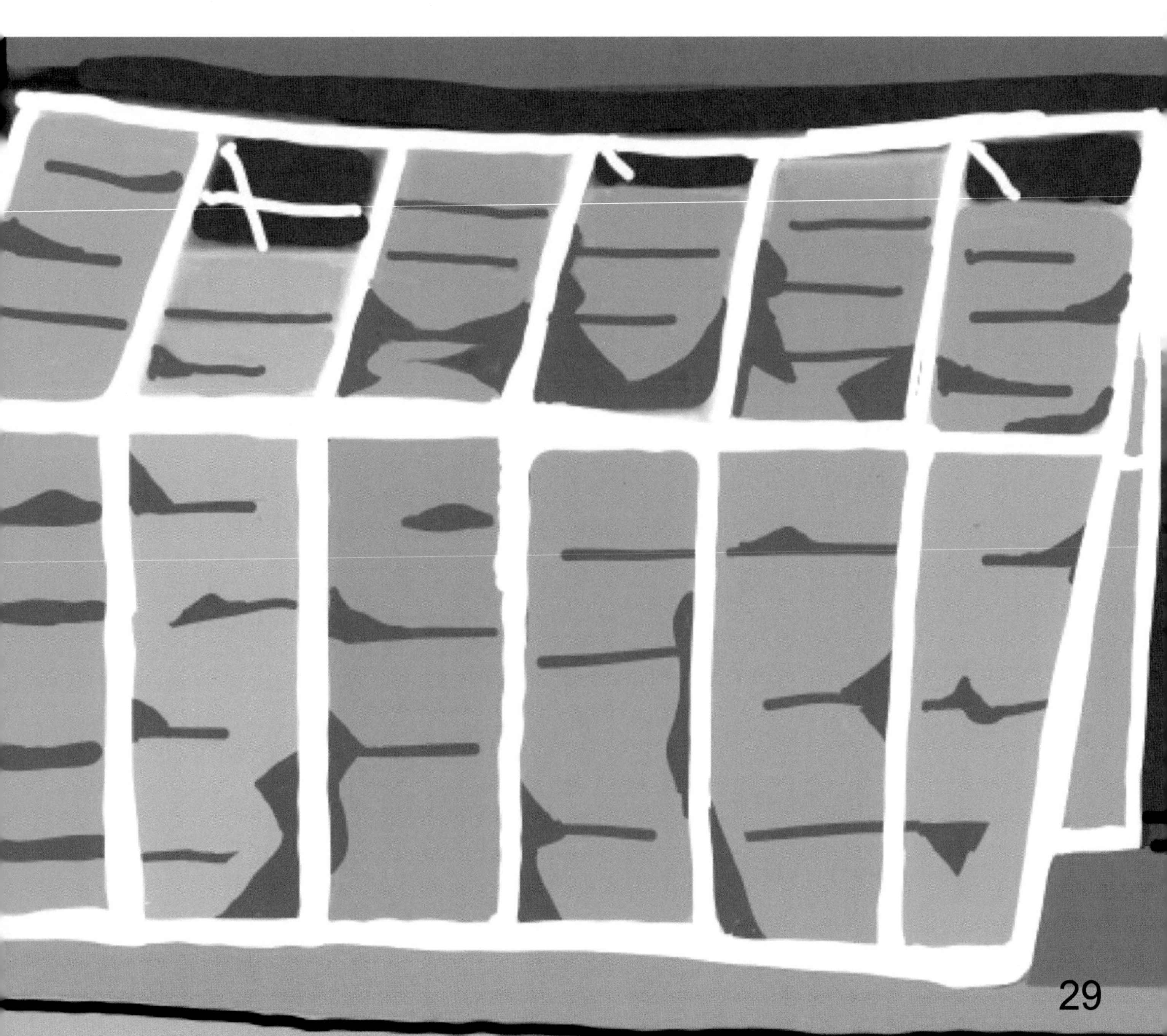

Blake didn't care.
She went under the benches that were in the doorway, and the other goslings followed her.
Then she waddled on top of the roof pieces that had fallen to the ground.
She plopped down and started drinking the rain water that had collected in a plastic tile.

Then Duxberry started to drink.

Slurp. Slurp.

Then Dresden and Homestead started to drink.

Maybe *some* geese are smart.

A few days later,
a man put a blue pool on the roof.
It had a ramp of sand on the outside
and rocks on the inside.
The geese were going to have fun in that.

The people who visited also put a tarp over a bench,
so the goslings had a dry place to hide during storms.

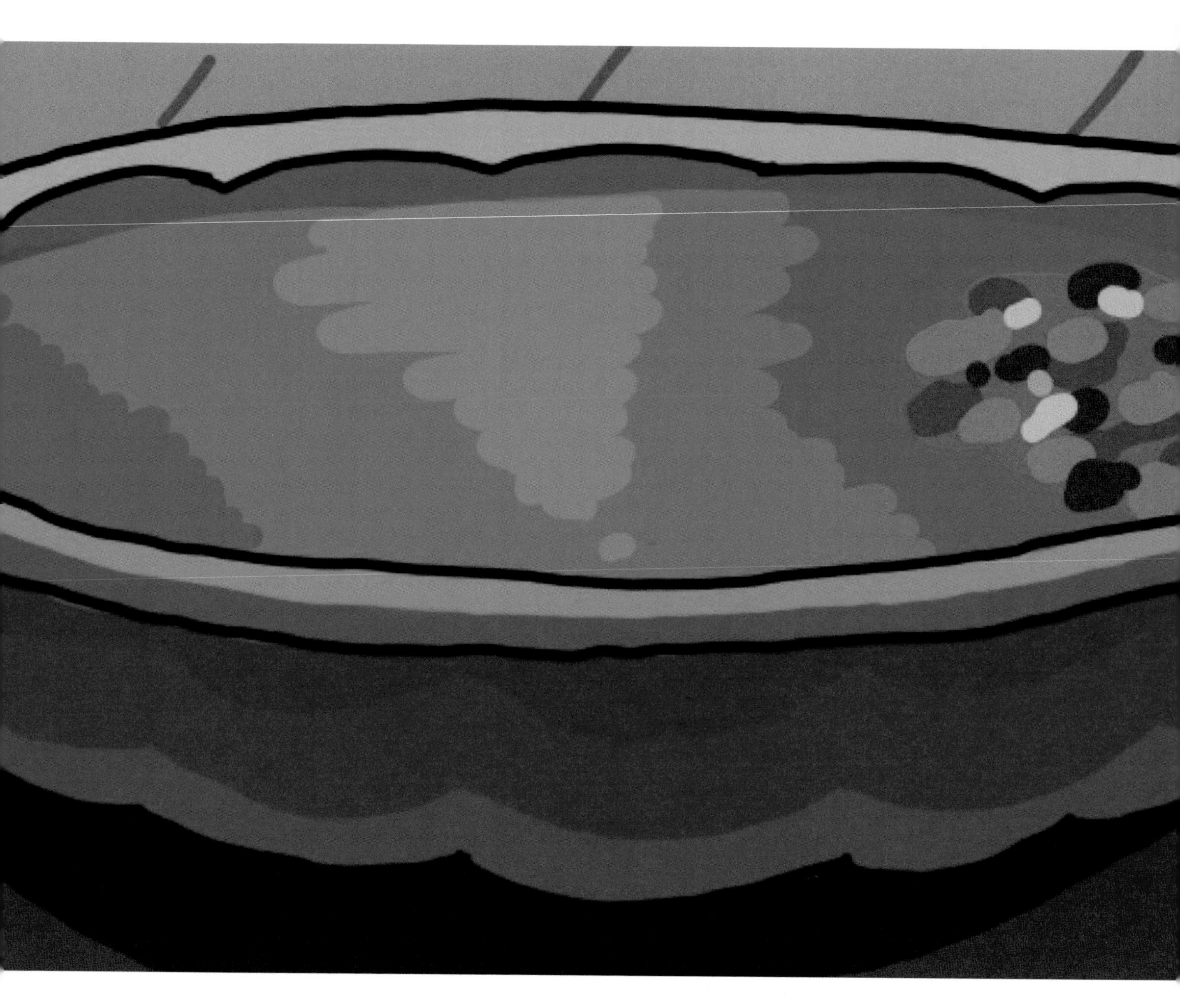

Every time visitors showed up,
they smiled, filled up the food,
cleaned out the water containers, and
took pictures of the geese.

Click.
Click.

And of course, they took pictures of us,
the tulips.
"I am famous!" I thought.
"They must know I saved the goslings."

Gander Goose was always
high up on the roof
hissing and honking when
people got too close.

However, Mother Goose
seemed relaxed
after a while.
One day a visitor spread
something around the green
roof.

I didn't know what it was
until she got close.

“Grass seeds?” I said.

“Oh no,” I thought. “They’re
never going to leave now.”

“These crazy people
actually like the geese,” I
whispered to my friends.

I watched the geese every
day for three months.
Blake explored every inch of
the green roof.

Dresden loved to hide under
benches, behind pots,
and even behind his parents.

Homestead wrapped his
neck around
anyone nearby for a quick
snuggle.

And Duxberry loved the
water. She played in the
pool, she dunked her head in
puddles, and she played in
the rain.

I thought back to when I heard the first, "Honk! Honk!"
I didn't sleep for days because I was so terrified.
Now, I see them learning to fly
and becoming independent.
Soon, they will be ready to start their new adventures
as a flock.

Soon, they will
be gone.

And I will be
sad.

Because I will
have
the empty
space
I *thought*
I wanted.

Canada Geese Facts

- It is against U.S. federal law to hurt a Canada Goose, eggs or nest, even if it is on your property.
- The female is called a goose, the male is a gander, and the babies are goslings.
- They are loyal. They usually mate for life. An injured goose is rarely left alone by other geese.
- After a goose and a gander mate, the females lay eggs some time in March-April, usually near water.
- One egg is laid approximately every 1.5 days. However, incubation does not occur until a goose starts sitting on the eggs. The eggs take about 28 days to hatch.
- Both parents protect the nest and goslings, but the gander is the main guard.
- Goslings can swim, walk and eat within a day of hatching.
- Water is important to geese because they use it to clean themselves and to drink.
- Goslings can dive about 30 feet into the water within a day or two of hatching.
- Waterproofing oils from the mother rub off onto the goslings to protect them from getting waterlogged and cold after a swim.
- Geese eat plants, nuts, seeds, bugs, and fruit. They love blueberries.
- Bread is not good for geese. The best food for geese is fresh grass.
- One goose can eat up to four pounds of grass in a day.
- Goslings can't fly until they are about 10 weeks old.
- Goslings will stay with their parents for one to two years. Females tend to stay longer than males.
- Geese have excellent memories and vision, and they see color better than humans.
- They fly in a V shape and take turns leading. They fly about 40 mph on average, but they are able to fly up to 70 mph with a good wind.
- They live, on average, 10-25 years.
- Once every year (usually in the summer), geese will molt their feathers and be unable to fly for about 6 weeks.
- When a goose honks or hisses, you are too close. You should remain calm and slowly back away. Do not turn your back on geese or run. Do not yell at or hit geese.

The real green roof geese

Made in the USA
Middletown, DE
09 November 2020

23367962R10022

ISBN 9798558441420
90000
9 798558 441420

LIBRARIAN LIV

WRITTEN BY: JOLEY VINEYARD ILLUSTRATED BY: JERRY VINEYARD

D1411309

WATCHING YOU GROW FROM THE LITTLE GIRL IN 1ST GRADE WITH THE GREATEST NUMBER OF A.R. POINTS IN THE SCHOOL TO THE SWEATER-WEARING BOOKER-LOVER YOU ARE TODAY HAS MADE MY HEART SO VERY HAPPY. KEEP READING, KEEP SHARING, AND KEEP POINTING TO HIM.

-MAMA GREENHEART

YOU HAVE GROWN INTO A BEAUTIFUL, INTELLIGENT WOMAN OF GOD AND IT HAS BEEN MY JOY TO BE YOUR DAD. I THANK THE LORD EVERYDAY FOR GIVING ME YOU. STAY FOCUSED ON JESUS AND BRUSH YOUR TEETH BECAUSE YOU ONLY GET ONE SET. I LOVE YOU MONKEYBRAINS!!!

-DANNO

LIBRARIAN LIV

WRITTEN BY: JOLEY VINEYARD
ILLUSTRATED BY: JERRY VINEYARD

THE PURR OF AN ENGINE AND THE WHEELS SPINNING ROUND WAS HEARD THROUGHOUT READ-NO-MORE, A GLUM LITTLE TOWN.

DOODADS
READ-NO-MORE LIBRARY

SHE PUSHED ON THE BRAKES AND CAME TO A STOP
AND GRABBED A BOOK FROM THE SHELF AND GAVE A SMALL HOP.

AS SHE LOOKED ALL AROUND, HER HEART DROPPED QUITE A BIT
AS READING WAS SOMETHING THAT THIS TOWN HAD QUIT.

THEIR FACES WERE SLACK IN FRONT OF THE SCREENS,

AND THEIR BRAINS HAD STOPPED THINKING IMAGINATIVE THINGS.

WEE-CUBES, AND X-BOTS, AND VIDEO PADS

AND TELLY-PHONES, TVS, AND OTHER DOODADS

HAD REPLACED ALL THE STORIES AND REPLACED ALL THE FUN

THAT READING COULD BRING TO EACH LITTLE ONE.

STEVENSON
DAHL
DiCAMILLO
VINEYARD
THE GIVING TREE
LITTLE WOMEN
PORTER
INDY
OTIS
X-BOT

NO ONE REMEMBERED RAMONA OR ANNE.
FORGOTTEN WAS NANCY AND CADDIE AND SAM.

AN ISLAND OF DOLPHINS AND A FRANKWEILER FILE
WERE MISSING FROM MINDS OF EACH TINY CHILD.

"I SHALL REMIND THEM OF READING AND THE JOYS THAT IT BRINGS.
I'LL REMIND THEM OF LIBRARIES AND BRING BACK THAT ZING!!

I SHALL TELL THEM OF KIPLING AND MILNE AND OF DAHL,
DICAMILLO AND BLUME AND THE REST OF THEM ALL."

WITH A BOOK IN HER HAND AND SUCH HOPE IN HER HEART
THAT LIBRARIAN LIV FILLED HER LIBRARY CART.

SHE FILLED IT WITH JUNIE AND THOSE BOXCAR KIDS.
SHE FILLED IT WITH BOOKS ABOUT YETIS AND SQUIDS

THE CLASSICS AND HUMOR AND SOME MYSTERIES
AND THRILLERS AND ROMANCE AND GOOD POETRY

SELF-HELP AND SCIENCE AND FAIRYTALES, TOO.
WHERE SOME PRINCES FIND LOVE WITH A LITTLE GLASS SHOE.

YETIS
CHARLOTTE'S WEB
PETERPAN
THE SECRET GARDEN
CINDERELLA

Librarian Liv left her sweet little Pearl,
the library bus she drove 'cross the world.

She found her a spot and settled on down and
invited the kids from all over town.

She convinced them to put down their machines
and enter new worlds without using screens.

THEY ENTERED A LAND WHERE MEATBALLS RAINED DOWN
AND A PIG FARM WITH SPIDERS WHERE FRIENDSHIPS ABOUND.

THEY TRAVELED TO WHERE THE SIDEWALK ENDS
AND WHERE TIME HAD A WRINKLE AND FROG AND TOAD WERE GOOD FRIENDS.

TO A SECRET GARDEN AND HOUSE ON THE PRAIRIE
AND ONWARD TO NEVERLAND, A PLACE WITH A FAIRY.

THEIR MINDS RACED WITH WILD THINGS AND UNSELFISH TREES
AND INDIANS IN CUPBOARDS AND MICE WITH COOKIES.

SOME
BOOK

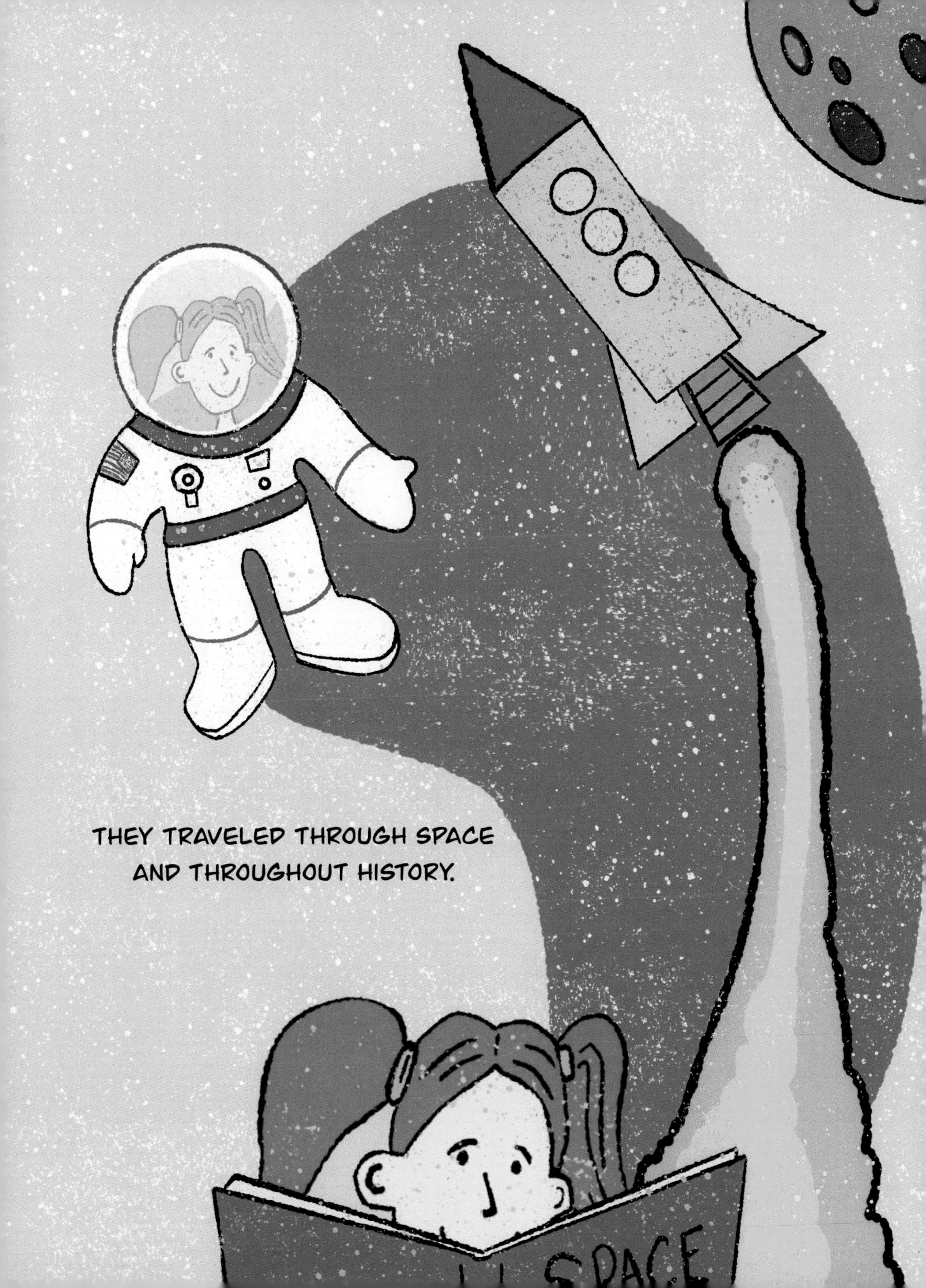
THEY TRAVELED THROUGH SPACE
AND THROUGHOUT HISTORY.
SPACE

THEY WALKED WITH EXPLORERS
THROUGH NEW TERRITORIES.
EXPLORERS

SHE READ TO THEM SEUSS AND SHE READ TO THEM GRIMM,
AND SHE REMINDED THOSE LITTLE HERS AND THOSE HIMS

THAT READING WAS MAGICAL, A WONDERFUL TIME,
AND THAT SPENDING YOUR DAY WITH A BOOK WAS SUBLIME!

HER STORY TIME GREW A LITTLE EACH DAY.
THEY'D SIT AT HER FEET AND BEG HER TO STAY.

THEY LOVED THAT TRAVELING BOOK-READING GIRL
WITH HER PUPPETS AND FELT BOARDS AND HER LIBRARY, PEARL!

READ-NO-MORE LIBRARY
YETIS
PETERPAN

PEARL

SOME OF THOSE KIDS THOUGHT THAT READING WAS TOUGH
BUT PRACTICED UNTIL IT WAS NO LONGER SO ROUGH!

THEY REALIZED THAT ENTERING THE WORLDS ON A PAGE
COULD UNLEASH THEIR MINDS FROM A LIMITED CAGE.

AND DO YOU KNOW WHAT HAPPENED TO THOSE LITTLE GUYS?
LISTENING TO LITERATURE HAD OPENED THEIR EYES!

THEY BEGAN TO CHECK OUT THEIR OWN LITTLE BOOKS,
AND READ FROM THEIR OWN SMALL COZY NOOKS.

THEY READ NEW ADVENTURES AND THEY READ OF THE PAST,
AND THEIR READING IMPROVED AND IMAGINATIONS GREW VAST.

VOCABULARIES GREW LARGER AND THEIR NEURONS SYNAPSED,
AND THE TIME BETWEEN USING THEIR GADGETS HAD LAPSED.

THE LIBRARY FOUND THAT NEW CUSTOMERS HAD COME.
WHAT'S BEST IS THEY FOUND THAT THE NEW ONES WERE YOUNG!

CHILDREN WERE BROWSING THE BOOKSHELVES ONCE MORE.
THEY WERE SITTING ON BEAN BAGS AND FILLING THE FLOORS!

AS LIBRARIAN LIV LOOKED AROUND WITH SUCH PRIDE
SHE CLOSED HER EYES AND BREATHED IN AND SIGHED.

"MY JOB HERE IS FINISHED. THE BOOKS HAVE ALL WORKED.
THESE CHILDREN NOW HAVE BRAINS THAT HAVE PERKED!

THEY'RE IMAGINING AND REFLECTING, AND RESEARCHING, TOO.
THEY'RE LEARNING OF OLD THINGS. THEY'RE LEARNING OF NEW.

THEY ARE FILLING UP JOURNALS WITH THEIR OWN CREATIONS,
AND WILL ONE DAY BECOME THEIR OWN WRITING SENSATIONS!"

READ-NO-MORE CHANGED ITS OUTDATED NAME
TO READ-TO-US-MORE WHICH THEY COULD PROUDLY PROCLAIM!

THE EMBRACED THEIR NEW LOVE OF BEING GREAT READERS,
KNOWING FULL-WELL THEY WERE CREATING GREAT LEADERS.

BOOKS
WELCOME BACK!!!

WELCOME
to
READ-TO-US-MORE
USA

SHE SHELVED ALL THE BOOKS AND SHE LOADED HER BUS
AND LEFT THE SMALL TOWN WITH NEW BOOKS TO DISCUSS.
SHE HEADED OUT WEST AND JUST COULDN'T WAIT
TO MEET THE NEXT TOWN AND HELP OUT ITS FATE.
THAT LIBRARIAN LIV CAN BE FOUND FAR AND WIDE
REMINDING THE CHILDREN, "LET BOOKS BE YOUR GUIDE!"
IF YOU'RE LUCKY SOMEDAY, YOU MAY SEE HER OUT,
SHE'LL BE SITTING AND READING TO CHILDREN, NO DOUBT!
PEARL
LEAVING
READ-TO-US-MORE
POP: 4,221

OTHER BOOKS MENTIONED IN THIS BOOK:

NANCY DREW MYSTERIES (CAROLYN KEENE)
CADDIE WOODLAWN (CAROL RYRIE BRINK)
THE CAT IN THE HAT (DR. SEUSS)
FROM THE MIXED-UP FILES OF MRS. BASIL E. FRANKWEILER (E. L. KONIGSBURG)
RAMONA QUIMBY (BEVERLY CLEARY)
ANNE OF GREEN GABLES (LUCY MAUD MONTGOMERY)
CLOUDY WITH A CHANCE OF MEATBALLS (JUDI BARRETT)
THE GIVING TREE / WHERE THE SIDEWALK ENDS (SHEL SILVERSTEIN)
CHARLOTTE'S WEB (E.B. WHITE)
A WRINKLE IN TIME (MADELEINE L'ENGLE)
ISLAND OF THE BLUE DOLPHINS (SCOTT O'DELL)
INDIAN IN THE CUPBOARD (LYNNE REID BANKS)
JUNIE B. JONES (BARBARA PARK)
THE BOXCAR CHILDREN (GERTRUDE CHANDLER WARNER)
FROG AND TOAD (ARNOLD LOBEL)
THE SECRET GARDEN (FRANCIS HODGSON BURNETT)
LITTLE HOUSE ON THE PRAIRIE (LAURA INGALLS WILDER)
PETER PAN (J.M. BARRIE)
WHERE THE WILD THINGS ARE (MAURICE SENDAK)
IF YOU GIVE A MOUSE A COOKIE (LAURA NUMEROFF)

AUTHORS MENTIONED IN THIS BOOK:

A.A. MILNE
ROALD DAHL
KATE DICAMILLO
JUDY BLUME
RUDYARD KIPLING
THE GRIMM BROTHERS

WELCOME BACK!!!
YETIS
PETERPAN
LEAVING
READ-TO-US-MORE
POP: 4,221
PEARL

WELCOME BACK!!!
YETIS
PETERPAN
LEAVING
READ-TO-US-MORE
POP: 4,221
PEARL

Made in the USA
Middletown, DE
27 December 2021

LIBRARIAN LIV

CHILDREN HAVE FORGOTTEN THE JOY OF FALLING INTO A GOOD BOOK SINCE TECHNOLOGY HAS TAKEN OVER. JOIN LIBRARIAN LIV AND HER BOOKMOBILE, PEARL, AS THEY TRAVEL TOWN TO TOWN REMINDING CHILDREN OF GREAT BOOKS, GREAT AUTHORS, AND GREAT TIMES!